Volcano Rescue!

A Tonka Joe® Adventure

by Michael Teitelbaum • Illustrated by Marty Roper

ISBN 0-439-25911-8

TONKA® and TONKA JOE® are trademarks of Hasbro, Inc.
Used with permission.
Copyright © 2001 Hasbro, Inc.
All rights reserved. Published by Scholastic Inc.
SCHOLASTIC, CARTWHEEL BOOKS, and associated logos are trademarks and/or registered trademarks of Scholastic Inc.

10 9 8 7 6 5 4 3 2 1   01 02 03 04 05
Printed in the U.S.A.   40
First printing, May 2001

Cartwheel
·B·O·O·K·S·®
SCHOLASTIC INC.

New York   Toronto   London   Auckland   Sydney   Mexico City   New Delhi   Hong Kong

Tonka Joe, the world's greatest mechanic, was hard at work in his shop putting the finishing touches on a brand-new car he called the Path Cutter.

Joe's nephew, Stevie, was visiting. "Is this where you build all your mega-cool vehicles, Uncle Joe?" he asked, looking around the huge building.

"That's right, Stevie," Joe replied. "I can build just about anything right here."

Just then, Joe's niece, J.J., rushed in. J.J. helped Joe with his projects. She also did scientific experiments of her own.

"I'm not getting any readings from my geothermal energy experiment up on the mountain, Uncle Joe," J.J. explained. "I'm going up to the research cabin to see what's wrong."

"Can I come?" Stevie asked excitedly.

"Sure," replied J.J.

"You two be extra careful," Joe warned. "Call me if you need anything."

J.J. and Stevie climbed to the top of a mountain near Tonka Joe's workshop. There, they entered an old wooden cabin filled with computer equipment.

J.J. checked the readings on the computer's monitor. Suddenly the cabin began to shake.

"What's going on?" Stevie asked, grabbing onto a desk to stop himself from falling.

"According to these readings," J.J. said, "this mountain is really an old volcano. And it's getting ready to erupt! I've got to get a message to Uncle Joe!"

Back in Tonka Joe's workshop, the word "HELP" began to flash on J.J.'s computer.

BING! BING! BING! The computer chimed loudly enough to catch Joe's attention.

"A message for help?" Joe asked, staring at the monitor. "J.J. and Stevie must be in trouble!"

"Time to whip my new Path Cutter into action!" Joe shouted as he put down his torque wrench.

Firing up the Path Cutter's powerful engine, Joe sped from his shop, racing toward the volcano.

ZOOOOM!!!

The Path Cutter approached a lake.

No time to go around it, Joe thought. *I'll just have to make my own shortcut!*

He yanked a lever near the Path Cutter's gearshift. The speeding vehicle's tires inflated like four giant balloons, just as it hit the water.

SPLASH!

The Path Cutter glided swiftly across the surface of the lake like a racing speedboat.

A huge gorge loomed just ahead. "Time to catch some air!" Joe announced. He punched a button on the dashboard. Helicopter blades extended from the back of the Path Cutter.

"Request permission for takeoff!" Joe joked, flipping another switch.

The enormous propeller began to spin, just as the Path Cutter reached the edge of the gorge.

WHOOSH!

The vehicle lifted into the air, easily sailing across the deep canyon, and landed safely on the other side.

Back on top of the mountain, things had gotten worse. The rumbling volcano shook the cabin fiercely. The small wooden building began to fall apart. Inside, J.J. and Stevie clung to a beam, dangling helplessly.

"I'm slipping, J.J.!" cried Stevie. "I can't hold on any longer."

"You've got to hold on," J.J. replied. "I know Uncle Joe will be here soon."

"Did someone mention my name?" boomed a friendly voice.
"UNCLE JOE!! YOU MADE IT!!" J.J. and Stevie shouted.
The Path Cutter had zoomed straight up the side of the mountain and now sat outside the cabin.
"Come on in, there's plenty of room!" Joe said, opening the Path Cutter's door.

J.J. grabbed Joe's hand and scrambled into the car. "Now take my hand, Stevie," she offered.

Stevie hesitated. Then the volcano trembled again, shaking the cabin.

"1 . . . 2 . . . 3 . . . GO!" said Stevie, as he grasped J.J.'s outstretched hand and climbed into the Path Cutter.

As Stevie settled into his seat, the mountain shook again. Then the cabin collapsed and tumbled away down the side of the mountain.

The Path Cutter raced up the side of the volcano, using a cable and pulley system Joe had rigged up.

As the Path Cutter rested on the edge of the volcano, J.J. checked the screen on her laptop computer. "Bad news, Uncle Joe," she reported. "This volcano is going to overflow with lava in about ten minutes—and the lava will flow right down onto the town below!"

"I've got an idea," said Joe, turning the Path Cutter around. They roared down the mountain and back to Joe's shop. There, the world's greatest mechanic got right to work.

"First, I'll attach this spinning drill to the front of the Path Cutter," Joe explained as he worked furiously. "Next, I'll put these powerful rockets onto the drill. Now we're ready to roll."

"The volcano's going to blow in less than five minutes, Uncle Joe!" cried J.J.

"Hop in, kids," replied Joe, firing up the Path Cutter's engine. "We've got no time to lose!"

Joe, J.J., and Stevie raced back to the mountain, zooming straight up the side.

"You'd better slow down, Uncle Joe," warned J.J. "We're almost at the edge of the volcano!"

"We're not stopping," Joe explained. "Make sure you're both buckled in tight!"

As the car plunged toward the bubbling lava, Joe fired a grappling hook and cable off the back of the vehicle. The hook snagged on a rock and the car swung back. As it swung forward again, Joe fired the spinning drill and rockets at the far wall of the volcano.

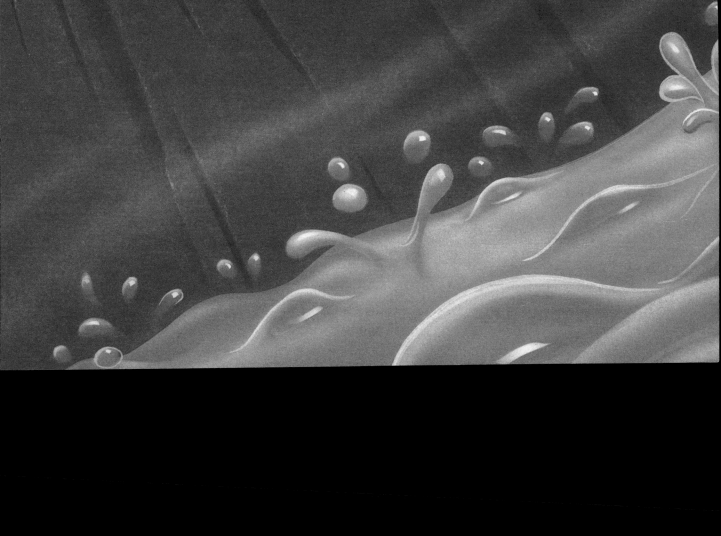

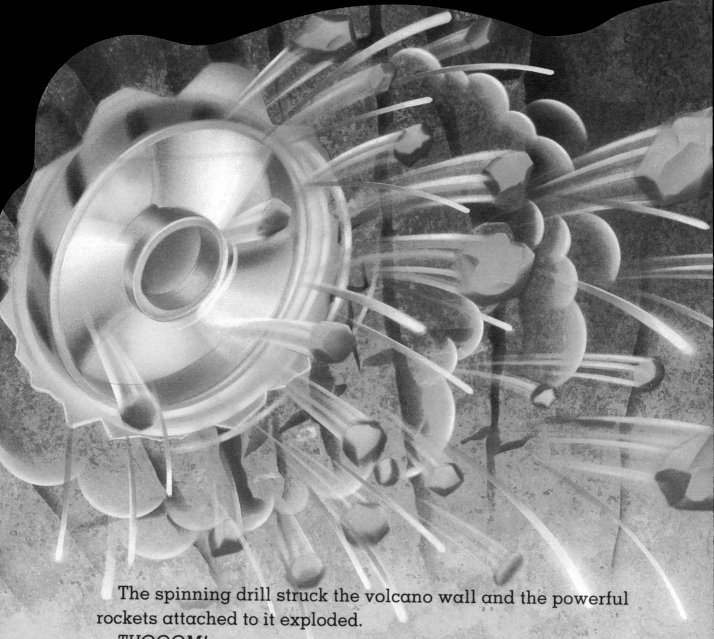

The spinning drill struck the volcano wall and the powerful rockets attached to it exploded.

THOOOM!

The rockets powered the drill, spinning it at an incredible speed, drilling a hole in the wall. The drill moved forward, carving out a tunnel through the volcano.

Joe released the grappling line from the back of the Path Cutter. The vehicle flew through the air and landed right in the tunnel on the far side of the volcano.

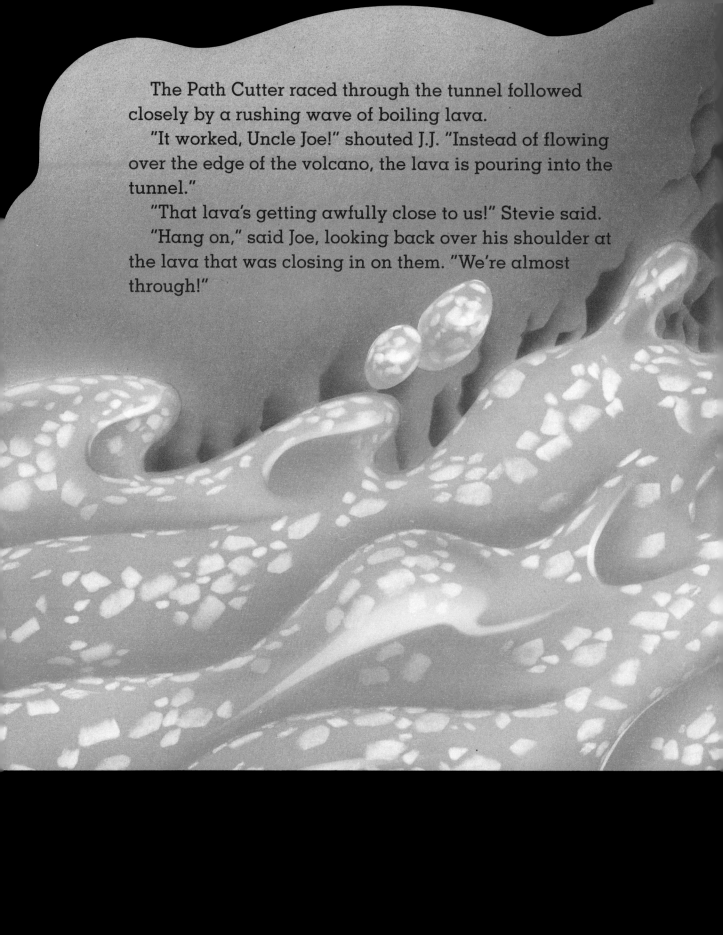

The Path Cutter raced through the tunnel followed closely by a rushing wave of boiling lava.

"It worked, Uncle Joe!" shouted J.J. "Instead of flowing over the edge of the volcano, the lava is pouring into the tunnel."

"That lava's getting awfully close to us!" Stevie said.

"Hang on," said Joe, looking back over his shoulder at the lava that was closing in on them. "We're almost through!"

FWOOOSH!

The drill blasted through the far side of the volcano wall, followed closely by the Path Cutter and the raging stream of lava. The lava poured into the lake at the base of the volcano.

"Great job, Uncle Joe!" said J.J. "The lava's stopping at the lake instead of hitting the town, and the volcano's settling down!"

"I have a question, Uncle Joe," Stevie said. "How do you land this thing?"

The Path Cutter's wheels extended and the vehicle came in for a landing—right at the starting line of a racetrack.

"Now let's see what this thing can *really* do. Hang on!" Joe shouted. He shifted, slammed down the accelerator, and peeled out down the track. *WHOOOSH!*